SCIENCE QUEST

The Search for

Better Conservation

by Carol Ballard

GARETH**STEVENS**
GS
PUBLISHING
A WRC Media Company

Please visit our web site at: www.garethstevens.com
For a free color catalog describing Gareth Stevens Publishing's list of high-quality books
and multimedia programs, call 1-800-542-2595 (USA) or 1-800-387-3178 (Canada).
Gareth Stevens Publishing's fax: (414) 332-3567.

Library of Congress Cataloging-in-Publication Data

Ballard, Carol.
    The search for better conservation / by Carol Ballard. — North American ed.
      p. cm. — (Science quest)
    Includes index.
    ISBN 0-8368-4553-6 (lib. bdg.)
    1. Nature conservation—Juvenile literature. I. Title. II. Series.
  QH75.B265   2005
  333.72—dc22   2004059133

This North American edition first published in 2005 by
Gareth Stevens Publishing
A WRC Media Company
330 West Olive Street, Suite 100
Milwaukee, WI 53212 USA

This U.S. edition copyright © 2005 by Gareth Stevens, Inc. Original edition copyright © 2004 by ticktock Entertainment Ltd.
First published in Great Britain in 2004 by ticktock Media Ltd., Unit 2, Orchard Business Centre, North Farm Road, Tunbridge Wells,
Kent, TN2 3XF.

Gareth Stevens editor: Jim Mezzanotte
Gareth Stevens designer: Kami M. Koenig

Photo Credits: (t=top, b=bottom, c=center, l=left, r=right)
Alamy: 1, 6 (b), 7, 15 (all), 22 (all). Frank Lane Picture Library: 2-3, 23 (all). Corbis: 10 (all), 11 (all), 14 (all), 16 (all),
17 (all), 18, 19 (all), 21 (c), 24, 25 (t), 28, 29 (all). IUCN: 8 (b), 9 (b). Natural History Museum: 5 (t). Science Photo Library:
4-5 (c), 5 (r), 9 (t), 20 (t), 21 (b), 26, 27 (all). PhotoDisc: 20 (b).

Printed in the United States of America

1 2 3 4 5 6 7 8 9 09 08 07 06 05

Contents

Words that appear in the glossary are printed in
boldface type the first time they occur in the text.

Every day, wild plants and animals face threats to their survival. These threats have become a serious problem. Many people are working hard to save Earth's plants and animals, as well as the places where they live. **Conservation** involves preserving plants, animals, and other natural resources on Earth.

Many Areas of Study

The main goal of a conservation scientist, also known as a conservationist, is to protect and save plants, animals, and **habitats** from damage, destruction, and **extinction**. People who work full time as conservation scientists usually train in one of the disciplines of **biology**, such as botany (the study of plants), **zoology** (the study of animals), **marine biology** (the study of life in the ocean), or **ecology** (the study of how the natural world works). They use their knowledge to work toward the conservation of plants, animals, and habitats in various parts of the world, especially in places that face the greatest threats, such as the Amazon **rain forest** in South America, which is threatened by logging. Since 1978, more than 190,000 square miles (500,000 square kilometers) of this forest have been destroyed.

Monitoring the numbers and sizes of species helps conservation scientists understand which animals are in danger.

One of the best known extinct creatures is the dodo. It was wiped out on its island home of Mauritius by human hunters.

Protecting Species

Some conservation scientists may work with a particular **species** to ensure that it does not actually become extinct. Animal and plant **breeding** programs may provide special assistance, care, and protection to allow young to be born, eggs to be hatched, and seeds to germinate. Ongoing care helps the young to survive to maturity and then to reproduce. If the species is no longer found living in the wild, scientists may try to find a suitable habitat for **reintroduction**, helping it until it is safely established and able to survive independently.

Collecting Data

The collection of information on changes in numbers of particular species of plants and animals over time is very important in conservation. This practice is called long-term monitoring. People of all ages can take part in local and national monitoring programs, and people interested in conservation may also join one of many national or international conservation organizations, such as the World Wide Fund for Nature (WWF). Money raised from the membership fees of these organizations goes towards conservation projects, and the organizations keep their members informed of current conservation problems and successes.

On the island of Surtsey, Iceland, created by a volcano in 1963, conservationists were able to monitor the arrival of several species to the island.

Changes and Challenges

The natural world is constantly changing. Today, however, many changes are due to the negative effects of human activity. The human population's growing need for food and space is having a huge effect on habitats around the world. Every day, for example, huge areas of forest are cleared for farming and hundreds of species become extinct. Conservationists seek to protect the natural world. They try to prevent habitat damage and the extinction of species due to human activity.

Natural Threats

Some threats to habitats are natural and cannot be avoided. **Droughts**, floods, and strong winds can damage large areas of land, affecting every kind of life. Earthquakes and volcanoes, though rare, can also have devastating effects. In 1883, for example, the Krakatoa volcano, on the Pacific island of Rakata, erupted. Explosions from the eruption were heard 2,200 miles (3,540 km) away in Australia, and all life on the island was wiped out by a layer of sterile ash. Since that time, biologists have been monitoring the **recolonization** of the island by plants and animals.

Researchers estimate that there are fewer than 2,500 tigers left in the world today.

Human Threats

More serious long-term threats are the result of human activities. The clearing of forests for timber, farming, and the construction of roads and buildings destroys natural habitats. This

SCIENCE CONCEPTS

Conditions for Life

All species have some basic needs for survival. They need a habitat to which they are suited (in the case of the polar bears shown at right, the Arctic), with an adequate food supply. They need to be safe from **predators** or anything else that could harm them, and they need to be able to reproduce successfully. If these basic needs are met, a species will survive. If any of the needs are not met, survival is unlikely. The numbers of stag beetles, for example, have declined rapidly as the beetles' natural habitat of dead wood has been cleared.

destruction is a serious problem, and so is the fragmentation of habitats. The clearing of land leads to habitats being broken up into smaller and smaller patches, or fragments. Large carnivores such as tigers require very large areas of forest to hunt for their food. If these areas are too small, the carnivores have trouble surviving. They may resort to hunting livestock on farmland, which can lead to conflict with people.

Changing Our Ways

Conservation organizations not only work to establish protected areas and save species, they also work to persuade governments to enact laws for the protection of habitats and individual species. Another important part of their work is to persuade companies in industries such as logging and oil production to modify the way they carry out their work, to reduce or eliminate harmful effects to the environment. Conservation organizations are also starting to work in partnership with people to help them manage their local natural resources.

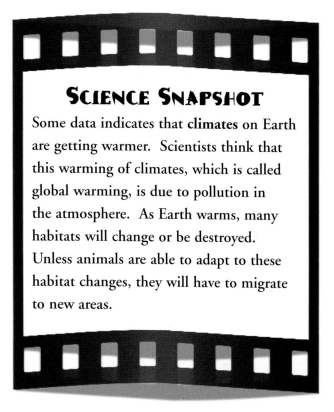

SCIENCE SNAPSHOT
Some data indicates that **climates** on Earth are getting warmer. Scientists think that this warming of climates, which is called global warming, is due to pollution in the atmosphere. As Earth warms, many habitats will change or be destroyed. Unless animals are able to adapt to these habitat changes, they will have to migrate to new areas.

Many people think that pollution from factories, cars, and other sources has caused the temperature on Earth to rise. This rise could eventually destroy many habitats.

Identifying Endangered Species

efore conservation scientists can begin to carry out any conservation work, they need to identify which habitats and living things are facing threats and what those threats are. Changes in the natural world often take place slowly, so conservationists try to monitor changes in habitats and their species over several years. The scientists then look for patterns in the data for clues about the risks that specific living things are facing or may face in the future.

The fate of the saiga antelope has fluctuated over the years and is now critical.

Assessing the Threat

In order to assess the risk of extinction and to be able to compare risks of extinction around the world, conservationists use a standardized system. They have designed a set of categories, known as the Red List categories, to assess the risk of extinction, with red representing danger. The International Union for the Conservation of Nature (IUCN), based in Geneva, Switzerland, maintains the international Red List. The Red List began in the 1980s, and new editions are now published each year on the Internet. The Red List gives information about all species known to be at risk of extinction.

Category	Description	Example
Critically **Endangered**	Extremely high risk of extinction	Leatherback turtle, giant ibis
Endangered	Very high risk of extinction in the wild	Swan goose, giant panda
Vulnerable	High risk of extinction in the wild	Cheetah, Himalayan black bear
Near Threatened	Could become threatened in the future	Green salamander
Extinct in the Wild	Only survives in botanic gardens or zoos	Red-tailed shark, Saharan oryx
Extinct	Does not survive anywhere	Martinique parrot, Falklands wolf

The Red List is published every year. It provides details on the state of all of Earth's threatened species.

SCIENCE CONCEPTS

Surveys

For **surveys** such as those carried out for the Red List (right) to be valid and useful, they have to be carried out scientifically. Observations and records must be precise and accurate. All aspects of the survey must be kept exactly the same every time observations are repeated, so that the only thing that changes is the number of individuals counted. This practice is similar to a scientific investigation in which scientists choose one variable that will change and keep everything else the same.

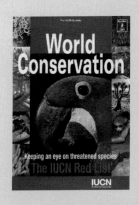

Changing Threats

In some cases, scientists are dispatched to a threatened habitat immediately to carry out surveys.

Just as the natural world constantly changes, so does the Red List change from one year to the next. Some species, for example, may be moved to a more serious category of threat, moving from "endangered" to "critically endangered." A good example of a change in the Red List is the saiga, a **nomadic** antelope that lives in Central Asia. For many years, it has been hunted for its meat and for the horns of the males, which are used in traditional Chinese medicine. From about 1 million animals in 1980, the saiga declined to about 180,000 in the year 2000. At this time, the saiga was categorized as "near threatened" on the Red List, but following further declines, its risk of extinction was upgraded to "critically endangered" in 2002. Species that are the focus of conservation efforts may be moved to a less threatened category or be removed from the Red List entirely.

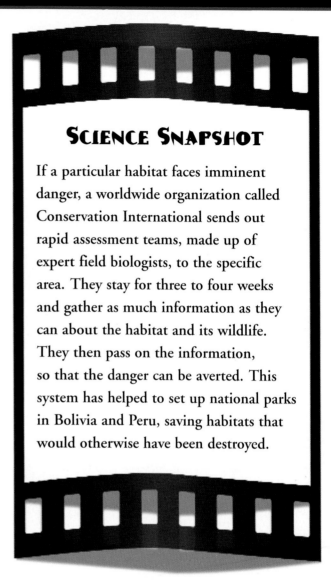

SCIENCE SNAPSHOT

If a particular habitat faces imminent danger, a worldwide organization called Conservation International sends out rapid assessment teams, made up of expert field biologists, to the specific area. They stay for three to four weeks and gather as much information as they can about the habitat and its wildlife. They then pass on the information, so that the danger can be averted. This system has helped to set up national parks in Bolivia and Peru, saving habitats that would otherwise have been destroyed.

The View from Space

Conservationists sometimes use **satellites** to gather information. By studying views of Earth's surface from space, they can monitor migration patterns and locate breeding grounds and winter homes. Entire habitats and environmental conditions can be monitored in this way. The use of satellites is an exciting development in conservation science and is set to expand in the future.

Conservationists look over a satellite map of a grizzly bear habitat in the Alberta foothills and Rocky Mountains.

One problem that conservation organizations, governments, and conservation scientists always face is finding enough money for the establishment of protected areas or for other forms of conservation. With money in short supply, all sites that require protection cannot be protected. Conservationists set priorities by deciding which areas are most in need of protection.

The island of Soqotra contains unique species of plants and is of particular value to conservationists.

Biodiversity and Endemic Species

Biodiversity refers to the number of plant and animal species in a particular place. Areas that are particularly rich in biodiversity, such as the **tropical** forests in the Amazon basin and in Southeast Asia, are of particular conservation importance and may require special protection. Some plants and animals are found only within a particular restricted place, such as in a certain mountain range or on a certain island. The island of Soqotra, for example, located off the eastern coast of Africa, has a high diversity of plant species; 35 percent of these species are **endemic** to the island and are found nowhere else in the world.

Ecoregions

The conservation organization WWF has created a conservation strategy based on the concept of ecoregions. An ecoregion is an area of land or water that contains a distinct grouping of plants and animals. WWF's Conservation Science Program has identified about 850 ecoregions around the world.

SCIENCE CONCEPTS

Identifying Species

Conservation scientists must be able to identify species that are threatened. Every distinct species has two **Latin** names. The first name is the **genus**, and the second name is the species. The tiger, for example, is *Panthera tigris*. Tigers from different areas may be slightly different in appearance. In this case, a **subspecies** name is used. The Siberian tiger, for example, is *Panthera tigris altaica*, and the Bengal tiger of India is *Panthera tigris tigris*.

Among these ecoregions, it has identified 200 **terrestrial**, freshwater, and marine ecoregions on the planet that are the most biologically distinct. WWF is focusing its conservation efforts in these areas.

Hot Spots

The conservation organization Conservation International has created a conservation strategy based on what are known as hot spots. A hot spot is an area of the world that has been reduced to less than 10 percent of its original vegetation and that contains the most threatened groups of plant and animal life on Earth. This strategy is based both on biodiversity and on the degree of threat, such as Red List status. The world's twenty-five most important global hot spots are one of Conservation International's main areas of focus for biodiversity conservation. One hot spot is the Western Ghats mountain range and tropical forest in southwest India.

▲ *Regions such as the Arctic, and the creatures that live there, are especially sensitive to change. These zoologists are taking samples from **tranquilized** polar bears to see if these bears have been affected by **pesticides** used in the area.*

▲ *New species of animals, such as this deep sea shrimp, are being found every year by conservationists.*

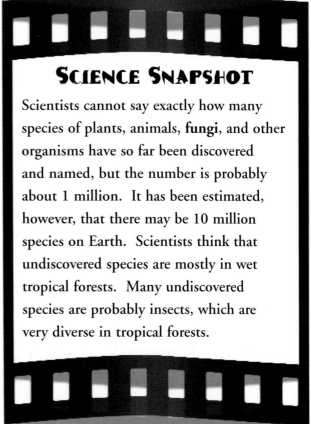

SCIENCE SNAPSHOT

Scientists cannot say exactly how many species of plants, animals, **fungi**, and other organisms have so far been discovered and named, but the number is probably about 1 million. It has been estimated, however, that there may be 10 million species on Earth. Scientists think that undiscovered species are mostly in wet tropical forests. Many undiscovered species are probably insects, which are very diverse in tropical forests.

Protected Areas

One of the main ways conservationists seek to protect the natural world is by the establishment of protected areas. In these areas, all living things are protected from hunting, **deforestation**, or other threats. The habitat of a protected area might be desert, woodland, wetland, or a coral reef in the ocean.

Types of Protected Areas

Protected areas can vary in size and have different forms of protection. The IUCN has created a system for categorizing protected areas. There are seven different types of protected areas. These types include a strict nature reserve, which is managed for scientific study or protection of its wilderness, and a managed resource protected area, which is managed for **sustainable** use of its natural resources.

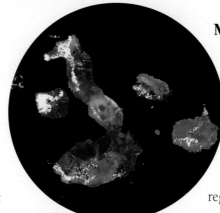

This satellite photo shows the protected Galapagos Islands as seen from space.

Methods of Protection

The first step in creating a protected area is usually getting laws passed for protection. After these laws are in place, rangers or guards usually monitor the area. These officials might carry out regular patrols of a protected area to prevent poaching, for example, and they may also be involved in monitoring the wildlife. Monitoring involves conducting surveys, or counts, of particular species to learn if there is an appropriate number of that species.

SCIENCE CONCEPTS

Science or Tourism?

Many people have different views about what should be preserved in a protected area. Some people think it is most important to focus on the beauty of an area, especially since the general public is most interested in attractive natural environments. The beauty of protected areas brings tourism and with it money. Many conservationists argue, however, that the entire ecosystem of an area is what matters most, including smaller, less attractive species such as grasses or insects, and that just protecting the more dramatic elements of an area creates an illusion of protection instead of a scientifically valuable natural area.

In some protected areas, such as areas of East Africa where people hunt elephants for their tusks, heavy poaching is a problem, and officials carry guns for their own protection.

Protecting Planet Earth

The percentage of Earth that is protected is increasing, but it is still small. By 2003, about 11.5 percent of the land area of Earth received some sort of protection. Less than 0.5 percent of the world's oceans, however, are protected. The two largest protected land areas are the Northeast Greenland IUCN Category II National Park of Greenland, with an area of 3,752 square miles (9,720 square kilometers), and the Ar'Rub al Khali Category VI Wildlife Management Area of Saudi Arabia, with an area of 2,470 square miles (6,400 sq km). The two largest marine protected areas are the Great Barrier Reef Category VI Marine Park of Australia, covering 1,329 square miles (3,444 sq km), and the Northwestern Hawaiian Islands Category VI Coral Reef Ecosystem Reserve, which has an area of 1,317 square miles (3,412 sq km).

Conservationists trying to protect the scarlet macaw have faced confrontations with armed poachers.

A ranger with the Kenyan Wildlife Service holds an elephant tusk confiscated from poachers.

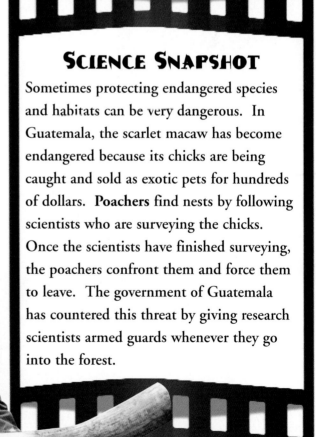

SCIENCE SNAPSHOT

Sometimes protecting endangered species and habitats can be very dangerous. In Guatemala, the scarlet macaw has become endangered because its chicks are being caught and sold as exotic pets for hundreds of dollars. **Poachers** find nests by following scientists who are surveying the chicks. Once the scientists have finished surveying, the poachers confront them and force them to leave. The government of Guatemala has countered this threat by giving research scientists armed guards whenever they go into the forest.

I n the past, many zoos simply kept animals in cages and charged people to see them. In recent years, however, many zoos have changed the way they care for and exhibit animals. Zookeepers now try hard to recreate conditions found in the animals' natural habitats, giving them more space and keeping them in groups rather than caged individually. Both zoos and **botanic** gardens also have new roles to play as places for the breeding of threatened animals and plants.

Snow leopards are bred in *captivity* to ensure the survival of the species.

Saving Species

Zoos and botanic gardens can be an important part of conservation efforts. Although conditions in a zoo or botanic garden can never be exactly the same as conditions found in the wild, these places do offer some benefits. Zoos can help ensure the survival of threatened species by providing them with a secure environment in which they can breed. Botanic gardens can offer a similar advantage for plants by providing the right soil and water conditions for growth.

A Helping Hand

Breeding programs can help increase the numbers of a threatened species. A well-known example is the success of zoos around the world in raising giant panda cubs. Another well-known example is the case of the Arabian oryx. The last few animals were captured in order to prevent them from being hunted. They bred successfully in captivity,

SCIENCE CONCEPTS

An Important Balance

Survival of a species depends on the balance between birth rates and death rates. For a population to remain stable, the rate of animals being born must be the same as the rate of animals dying. If the birth rate is higher than the death rate, which is the case with animals such as pigs (right) and rabbits, the population will expand and thrive. If the birth rate is lower than the death rate, which is the case with pandas, the population will shrink and eventually become endangered.

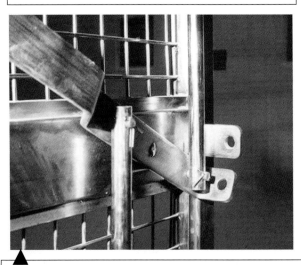

Giant pandas are so rare that zoos play a crucial role in preserving the species.

and they have now been reintroduced into the wild in several countries. From only a handful of oryx there is now a total of about 4,000, reintroduced into the wild and found in zoos worldwide.

Zoo Costs

The cost of maintaining a zoo's facilities, caring for its animals, and operating its breeding programs can be very high. Zoos use several methods for raising money. Most zoos charge the general public an entry fee to see the animals. Some zoos also run animal adoption programs, in which people provide money for the care of a particular animal. In some cases, zoos receive government funding. They may also operate as charities.

Many people feel uneasy about wild animals being kept behind bars in zoos, but zoos help prevent endangered species from becoming extinct.

SCIENCE SNAPSHOT

Many people think there is nothing wrong with keeping wild animals in zoos. Other people, however, think humans have no right to keep animals in captivity. The argument for and against zoos continues, as people try to balance animal rights and the idea that captivity is cruel against the benefits of regular feeding, safety from **predators**, **veterinary** care, and successful breeding programs.

Rare birds, such as this spectacular red kite, have been released back into the wild after successful zoo breeding programs.

Invasive Aliens

All animals and plants **evolve** in a particular place and then spread naturally. The speed and efficiency of modern transportation, however, has led to some species being carried around the world and introduced to places where they are not naturally found. A plant or animal introduced, either deliberately or accidentally, to a habitat to which it is not **native** is known as an **alien species**.

Invasive Species

In many cases, the introduction of an alien species has little effect on the habitat to which it is introduced. Some species, however, especially those that are able to reproduce quickly and in large numbers, become **invasive** and are then known as invasive alien species. One example of such a species is the small Indian mongoose, which eats other small animals. It was introduced to sugar cane plantations on the Pacific islands of Fiji so it would eat rats that were plaguing the sugar cane crop. Unfortunately, the mongooses discovered that the native lizards and frogs on the island were easier to catch, and they mostly ignored the rats.

The introduction of small Indian mongooses to Fiji backfired when the animals preyed on lizards and frogs instead of the rats they had been brought in to catch.

New Problems

Invasive alien species can be a serious threat to other **organisms**. The Indian mongooses, for example, preyed on lizards and frogs that lived on the ground instead of in trees and so were easy to catch. These lizards and frogs were driven to extinction on several Fijian islands. Plants that are very hardy and produce many seeds can, in the wrong place, cause harm, and so can other types of organisms. In the early twentieth century, for example, a fungul disease known as chestnut **blight** was accidentally introduced to North America from Asia. The fungus nearly drove the American chestnut tree to extinction.

SCIENCE CONCEPTS

The Spread of Alien Species

Organisms can be carried around the world in many ways. Ships that transport heavy cargo, for example, take in water as **ballast** for a return journey. A ship may take in ballast water in the Indian Ocean and then sail to the Atlantic Ocean. Before crew members load new cargo, they have to empty the ballast water. This ballast water may contain alien marine species from the Indian Ocean. In some cases, species have been introduced deliberately to another habitat.

The freshwater zebra mussel has invaded waterways in North America, posing a multibillion dollar threat.

SCIENCE SNAPSHOT

In the last hundred years, more than 4,500 foreign plants and animals have settled in the United States. The cost of invasive species to the U.S. economy is $137 billion per year. Invasive species have also hurt the country's endangered native species, causing these species to decline by nearly 50 percent. Invasive species threaten nearly two-thirds of the habitats of the country's endangered species, causing 3 million acres (1.2 million hectares) of habitats to be lost every year.

Combating Alien Species

The best way to stop foreign species from settling in an area is to prevent them from being brought to the area in the first place. Around the world, new laws have been put in place that make boat owners clean their boats thoroughly every time they travel. Ballast water exchange programs have also been established, to ensure that water from arriving boats is not dumped on foreign shores. If a species does become established in a new place, conservationists usually try to wipe out the species as quickly as possible. Conservationists in the United States are particularly worried about the Asian longhorned beetle settling in the country, and they have set up a hotline for anyone who spots one of these beetles so they can be destroyed quickly. In 2002, Maryland state authorities drained a lake to kill off the beetles after someone spotted them.

The spectacled caiman has been introduced to the United States from Central and South America. It now competes with native alligators for food.

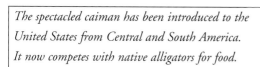

Reintroduction Efforts

As a result of the successful breeding in zoos of animals that are either extinct in the wild or reduced to very low numbers, there have been enough numbers of some species to allow reintroduction into the wild. Reintroduction usually takes place within a protected area, so the reintroduced animals will have a high chance of survival. One important goal of reintroduction is to give the animals the opportunity to breed so they will produce offspring born in the wild.

The Arabian Oryx

One well known and successful reintroduction is that of the white, or Arabian, oryx to several Arabian countries. In 1964, "Operation Oryx" captured the last few known wild oryx in southern Arabia on the border of Yemen and Oman. These animals were added to a few more oryx that were already in private zoos. This group, which became known as the World Herd, was moved to the Phoenix Zoo in the United States, where they were bred very successfully. In 1980, oryx were returned to Oman and released into an unfenced protected area. Oryx were able to roam freely in the wild once more. At a later date, oryx were also released into two protected areas in Saudi Arabia, one unfenced and one fenced.

After being bred in captivity, Arabian oryx were successful reintroduced into the wild.

SCIENCE CONCEPTS

Reintroduction Problems

When a species has become extinct in the wild, there are usually only a few animals in captivity from which to breed for reintroduction. The global population of about four thousand oryx are descended from only eight oryx, which means there are only eight types of **genetic** variation in the global oryx gene pool. When conservationists reintroduce oryx, they try to ensure that all eight original types of variation are present among the reintroduced animals.

Wolves in Yellowstone National Park

Northern Rocky Mountain wolves were native to Yellowstone National Park, in the western region of

Since 1995, wolves have again roamed through Yellowstone National Park.

the United States, when the park was established in 1872. Predator control was practiced in the park in the late 1800s and early 1900s, however, and by the 1970s, Yellowstone had no wolf population. In the 1990s, officials devised a plan to capture wolves in Canada and reintroduce them to Yellowstone. In 1995, fourteen wolves were released into the park, and in 1996, seventeen more wolves were released. The first fourteen wolves bore two **litters** totalling nine pups. In 1996, four packs of wolves produced fourteen pups. The return of this species, missing from the world's first national park for the past half century, has been a milestone in reintroduction efforts.

A Continuing Success Story

Today, nineteen species have been reintroduced into the wild after being bred in captivity. Some species, such as the Arabian oryx, American bison, red wolf, Pere David's deer, Guam kingfisher, Guam rail, and California condor, were extinct in the wild when the program began. Other species, including the bald eagle and the alpine ibex, have been put back into places where they used to live. The bald eagle can now be seen flying in the skies over Catalina Island, off the coast of California, for the first time in decades.

SCIENCE SNAPSHOT

The Millennium Seed Bank Project is a global conservation project based in London. The project's botanists seek to collect and conserve seeds from thousands of plant species worldwide. They also want to research and improve seed conservation, provide seeds for botanical research, and be able to reintroduce species back into the wild. The project should ensure the survival of plant species that might otherwise become extinct.

In 1987, the last few wild California condors were captured and put into a breeding program at the Los Angeles Zoo and the San Diego Wild Animal Park.

Into the Future

Today, people are much more aware of environmental and conservation issues than they were in the past. Many people try hard to protect and conserve the living things around them. Scientists are constantly discovering new species and developing better ways of safeguarding the resources of the natural world.

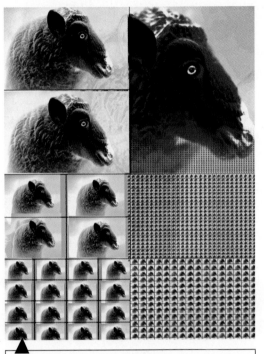

The possibilities of cloning may prove a way to save endangered species in the near future.

Using Science and Technology

Some of the most exciting developments in conservation science are in the field of genetics, the study of inherited **traits**. Geneticists have developed ways of taking a cell from an organism and **cloning** it to produce a new, genetically identical organism. Cloning could be very important in saving an endangered species from extinction, because it could provide a way of increasing the population of a species. Modern technology, though developed for other purposes, can often help conservation efforts. Satellite tagging, for example, can be used to track individual animals. In New Zealand, tiny **transmitters** have been attached to dolphins' fins. They send out signals that are detected by satellites, which then send information about the dolphins' location back to scientists on Earth. Some conservationists, however, argue that implanting the transmitters causes the dolphins more stress than the information is worth.

SCIENCE CONCEPTS

People vs. Habitats

Around the world, human activity is causing the destruction of habitats. In poor countries, habitats are often exploited for the valuable resources they contain. International cooperation and financial support will be needed to stop this exploitation. In richer countries, habitats are often destroyed as populations expand. **Pollution** is another serious problem. Governments will need to decide how to balance the needs of people with the needs of the natural world.

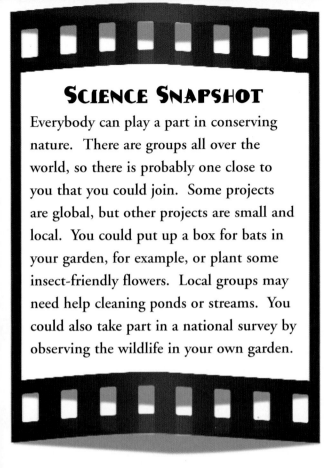

SCIENCE SNAPSHOT

Everybody can play a part in conserving nature. There are groups all over the world, so there is probably one close to you that you could join. Some projects are global, but other projects are small and local. You could put up a box for bats in your garden, for example, or plant some insect-friendly flowers. Local groups may need help cleaning ponds or streams. You could also take part in a national survey by observing the wildlife in your own garden.

Learning from the Past

Some government leaders recognize the damage that people have done to the natural world in the past. By working together, and listening to advice from conservation scientists, these leaders are trying to find ways of ensuring that such damage is not repeated. In many countries, natural habitats are destroyed as people build new roads, towns, and factories. At the same time, old buildings in city centers are often demolished. People are now being encouraged to rebuild on the sites of old buildings (brownfield sites) instead of using up any more countryside (greenfield sites).

Changing How We Live

Laws may have to be passed to prevent damage to the environment. If there are severe penalties for breaking these laws, people may be less likely to do so. In other cases, education may help. If people know about the effects their actions may have on the natural world and understand about conservation issues, they may choose to live their lives in a more environmentally friendly way.

Planting your garden with flowers that bloom and produce nectar can attract an array of beautiful butterflies.

Two conservationists look at reseeded grazing lands over an unused open-pit mine in the United States.

21

Case Study: Whales

Whales are amazing creatures. Although whales live in water, they are mammals, not fish, so they have lungs and breathe air. Whales are also **warm-blooded**. Instead of laying eggs, they give birth to live offspring that suckle milk from their mothers. Marine biologists use **aerial** surveys, satellite tracking, photo identification, and deepwater videoprobes to gather data about whales.

The number of whaling ships has decreased in recent years.

Blue Whales

Between 1904 and 1967, more than 350,000 blue whales were killed in the Southern **Hemisphere**. In 1967, the whales were given legal protection, but some countries did not agree to the protection and continued whaling. Today, blue whales still need protection. The whales are rarely hunted now, but they face other threats. They rely on **plankton** for their food, and many marine biologists think that, if climate changes continue, this food may become scarce. A lack of food would lead to many blue whales dying. Several international organizations have been established to protect and conserve blue whales and to enable people everywhere to find out more information about them.

Rescue Response

Every year, many whales swim too close to shore and become stranded. In Scotland, a special whale and dolphin ambulance is now in use. This truck has been specially adapted to carry vital equipment that can help rescuers locate, treat, and re-float stranded whales. Many whales die after colliding with ships or becoming tangled in fishing gear. A plan is now being developed for reducing these accidents off the coasts of the United States. Buoys will be fitted with electronic equipment, including transmitters and hydrophones, which are instruments that detect underwater sounds. The buoys will detect whale sounds and transmit information about the location of whales to ships in the area. The ships can then avoid the whales.

Some people from traditional whaling communities argue it is their right to continue to hunt whales.

This humpback whale was photographed near Hawaii.
Hunting has drastically reduced the number of these whales.

- There are two groups of whales, toothed whales and baleen whales.
- Blue whales are the largest creatures living on Earth.
- If whales swim too close to the shore, they may become stranded on the beach.
- In some places, blue whale populations are now growing in size.
- Climate change may lead to many blue whales dying from lack of food.

In the past, whales were hunted for their **blubber** and for their bones, which were used as tools and building materials.

Case Study: Gorillas

Gorillas are the largest of the great apes and can live to be about fifty years old. These animals share many of the characteristics of humans. In fact, the name gorilla means "hairy person." Gorillas use their faces to express emotions, and, like humans, their faces are different from one another. The unique faces of these apes enable zoologists to identify and monitor individual gorillas.

A Variety of Gorillas

There are two species of gorilla, eastern gorillas and western gorillas. Each species can be divided into two smaller groups. Eastern gorillas consist of mountain gorillas and Grauer's gorillas. Western gorillas consist of western lowland gorillas and Cross River gorillas. All gorillas are endangered. Mountain gorillas, however, are the most at risk and are on the verge of becoming extinct. Also called "cloud gorillas," they live high in mountain forests. They are found only in a small area in central Africa, on the Virunga volcanic mountains, which span the countries of Uganda, Rwanda, and the Democratic Republic of Congo.

Many Threats

Gorillas face several threats to their survival. Their habitats are shrinking due to agriculture and logging. In addition, their habitats have been destroyed by wars. Poachers hunt gorillas, killing them for the "bushmeat" trade. No mountain gorillas are held in captivity in any legal zoo or private collection anywhere in the world. Some people, however, have killed female gorillas and taken their babies, which are then sold illegally as pets.

Gorillas have distinctive faces, just like humans. They sometimes act like humans, too.

Logging has destroyed many of the mountain gorillas' habitats.

Rescue Effort

Some groups of people are working hard to save mountain gorillas. The Virunga National Park offers some habitat protection and safety from poachers. The International Gorilla Conservation Program (IGCP) has set up a ranger-based monitoring system to collect data and provide help in areas where it is most needed. Fierce fighting in the areas in which the gorillas live, however, has disrupted conservation efforts, because many rangers and park wardens have been in danger and have been unable to continue their work. Maps of the Virunga National Park are out of date, making it difficult to monitor the gorillas accurately. New information systems that rely on satellites are being used to produce up-to-date maps of the park. With these new information systems, scientists can predict future changes and outcomes, which will help them to plan effective long-term strategies for helping the gorillas.

Case Study Fact File

- All gorillas are endangered.
- A male gorilla is twice the size of a female gorilla.
- The gorilla's only enemies are leopards and humans, but crocodiles can be dangerous to lowland gorillas.
- The habitats of mountain gorillas are threatened because the rich volcanic soil is highly valued for farming.
- Mountain gorillas do not reproduce quickly. Females give birth for the first time at about age ten and will have more offspring every three or four years.

Western Lowland Gorilla

Mountain Gorilla

Eastern Lowland Gorilla

Today, gorillas are found in only a few areas of Africa.

Case Study: Golden Sun Moth

T he golden sun moth used to be widespread in Australian grasslands, living among wallaby grass and spear grass. Today, however, only about 1 percent of this grassland remains. Some grassland has been destroyed by spreading towns. Agriculture has also destroyed much of the grassland, through wetland drainage, tree planting, overgrazing, and the use of pesticides and **fertilizers**. Golden sun moths are now found only in a few small, isolated areas.

Life Cycle of the Moth

Entomologists studying the golden sun moth do not know all the details of its life cycle, but they think it probably lasts two to three years. Female sun moths lay eggs between plants and the soil. After hatching, the **larvae** tunnel into the plant, feeding on the plant tissue. The larvae then build short, silk-lined tunnels into the soil to feed on roots. A larva becomes a **pupa**, from which an adult moth emerges. Adult moths only survive for about two days. In this short period of time, eggs are laid to start the next generation. If anything happens to the adults during their short lives, however, eggs are not laid and there can be no next generation.

Habitat Management

The golden sun moth is critically endangered, but many people are working to ensure its survival. Surveys have been carried out to identify sites where colonies survive. Habitat management plans have been put into action to ensure that the areas of grassland suitable for the moths expand. Pesticides kill the moths, so farmers have been asked to avoid using pesticides at the times when the adult moths are flying and laying eggs. Female moths cannot fly very far, so they are unable to move from one site to another. Grassland areas are being planted to link isolated sites together, enabling the moths to breed more easily.

This scientist is extracting a sample of body fluid from a moth larva for genetic analysis.

The adult golden sun moth lives for just two days.

Captive Breeding

Another way to help ensure the survival of the golden sun moths involves the breeding of the moths in captivity. This breeding increases the number of moths so that some can be reintroduced to suitable natural habitats.

It also allows entomologists to study the moths very closely, so they will be able to understand the moth populations more fully. By looking at the genetic material of the moths, scientists can learn about how the moth populations have spread and separated. Scientists also hope that, by studying the golden sun moth, they will develop a greater understanding of other insect populations and the threats they face.

The Golden Sun Moth is found only in a few small areas of grassland in southeastern Australia.

NORTHERN TERRITORY

QUEENSLAND

WESTERN AUSTRALIA

SOUTH AUSTRALIA

NEW SOUTH WALES

ACT

VICTORIA

Case Study: Rain Forests

Rain forests are found in hot, damp tropical regions near the **equator**. They get at least 158 inches (4,000 millimeters) of rain every year and have no dry season, and they have an average daily temperature between 70° Fahrenheit (21°Celsius) and 81°F (27°C). More than half of the world's estimated 10 million species of plants and animals live in tropical rain forests, but vast areas of rain forests are destroyed every year. In less than fifty years, more than half of the world's tropical rain forests have been destroyed. The rate of destruction is still accelerating.

A Crucial Resource

Rain forests are often called "the lungs of the world," because trees and other plants in rain forests convert so much carbon dioxide into oxygen. When an area of rain forest is cleared, all living things in the area are affected. Animals cannot survive without their shelter and food sources. Native peoples who may have lived in the rain forest for thousands of years lose their homes and their natural ways of life. Some rain forest plants have been found to provide important medicines and foods. Many native people in rain forests are very knowledgeable about their lands and can guide scientists to new discoveries. As rain forests are destroyed, however, much of this knowledge is lost forever.

Trail of Destruction

Many rain forest trees are cut down for valuable hardwoods, such as mahogany. Cutting down trees in a rain forest leads to further destruction, as habitats vanish, soil is lost due to **erosion**, and the air and water are polluted. Lush, fertile lands are left bare and barren. If an area of rain forest is destroyed before scientists have had a chance to study it carefully, we may lose species that we never even knew existed.

Rain forests provide homes for many rare species, including the orangutan.

At least half of all the animal and plant species in the world live in rain forests.

Saving the Rain Forests

Conservationists are trying hard to save the rain forests. Providing information to people about the consequences of cutting down rain forest trees has helped to reduce demand for hardwoods. Financial assistance from other countries can help set up alternatives to logging in countries where logging is an important part of the economy. Some drug companies are investing in rain forest research with the goal of making new drugs from tropical rain forest plants.

Some researchers float over the forest to carry out their research.

This satellite picture shows a section of the Amazon rain forest. The light regions show areas of deforestation.

aerial: having to do with being up in the air.

alien species: a species that is introduced to a new region, often by humans, and which often has a harmful effect on species already living in the region.

baleen: a structure of plates that baleen whales have, instead of teeth, for catching food.

ballast: a substance, such as seawater, put in the hull of a ship for added stability.

biology: the study of life and living organisms

biodiversity: the number and variety of organisms found within a specified geographic region.

blight: a plant disease that results in the sudden wilting and dying of the affected parts

blubber: the fat of whales.

botanic: having to do with plants.

botanist: a person who studies plants.

breeding: the reproduction of organisms.

captivity: in the case of wild animals, the state of living in an enclosed area, such as a zoo.

climates: patterns of weather for a certain region recorded over a long period of time.

cloning: using information inside the cell of an organism to create another, genetically identical organism.

conservation: the protection, preservation, management, and restoration of wildlife and natural resources such as soil and water.

deforestation: the cutting down and clearing away of trees in an area.

droughts: periods of extremely dry weather.

ecology: the science of the relationships between organisms and their environments.

ecosystem: the organisms and environment of a particular area and the ways they interact.

endangered: likely to become extinct.

endemic: being native to, or found only in, a particular region.

entomologist: a scientist who studies insects.

equator: an imaginary circle around the middle of Earth, dividing it into the Northern Hemisphere and the Southern Hemisphere.

erosion: wearing away by wind and rain.

evolve: the process by which something changes very slowly over a long period of time.

extinction: the end of existence on Earth for a particular species.

fertilizers: substances that add nutrients to the soil to help plants grow.

fungi: plantlike organisms that must attach to other organisms to get food.

genetic: having to do with genes, which determine the traits of organisms that get passed down through the generations.

genus: a grouping of species that share some common characteristics.

habitats: the places where certain groups of organisms live.

hemisphere: the northern or southern half of Earth, as divided by the equator.

invasive: in the case of alien species, having spread thoughout a particular region and threatened the well-being of other species.

larvae: the early, wormlike form of an insect.

Latin: a language, originally created by Romans thousands of years ago, that is the basis for English and other modern languages and is used by scientists to name living things.

litters: groups of offspring born at the same time to the same mother.

marine biology: the study of living things in the ocean.

native: having occurred naturally in a region, instead of having arrived from another region.

nomadic: being an organism that roams over a large area and does not stay permanently in one particular place.

organisms: living things, such as plants, animals, or fungi.

pesticide: a chemical used to kill pests, such as insects that destroy crops.

plankton: microscopic organisms that live in water.

poachers: people who hunt animals illegally.

pollution: various substances, usually created by human activity, that can harm people, other living things, and natural resources.

pupa: the form an insect takes at that stage of its life cycle when it is changing into an adult.

predators: animals that kill and eat other animals.

rain forest: dense forest in tropical areas.

recolonization: the process by which a group of organisms once again populates an area.

reintroduction: the process of putting organisms back into natural habitats where they have not lived for an extended period of time.

satellite: a device launched into space that orbits Earth and can send back images of Earth's surface.

species: a group of organisms that has certain characteristics.

subspecies: a group of organisms with particular characteristics that make them different from other organisms of the same species.

surveys: processes by which information about something is gathered.

sustainable: able to continue over an extended period of time.

terrestrial: having to do with land.

traits: the characteristics of an organism.

tranquilized: having been made calm by the effects of a drug.

transmitter: an electronic device that sends a radio signal to another device.

tropical: having to do with the region of Earth's surface close to the equator, characterized by a warm, damp climate

veterinary: having to do with the health care of animals.

warm-blooded: able to maintain a constant internal body temperature that does not depend on the outside temperature.

zoology: the study of animals

Index